Grandma's House

To Sophie & Maddie~
Cherished memories last
forever!
~Dana Gambardella

Dana Gambardella
illustrated by Ross Chirico

Book Design by Jill Ronsley, Sun Editing & Book Design, suneditwrite.com

ISBN: 978-0-9993144-1-8
Library of Congress Catalog number: 2017953148
Published by Literacy Chef Publishing, LLC

Literacy Chef Publishing, LLC

North Providence, Rhode Island
Website: literacychefpublishing.com

10 9 8 7 6 5 4 3 2 1

Printed and bound in the USA

In loving memory of my grandmother,
Angela Gambardella,
And to my father, who never fails to pick me up.

Tranquility nourishes my soul whenever I'm at Grandma's house. The baseboard's constant buzzing carries heat throughout the room.

I glance
at the ornate
cuckoo clock
in the corner.

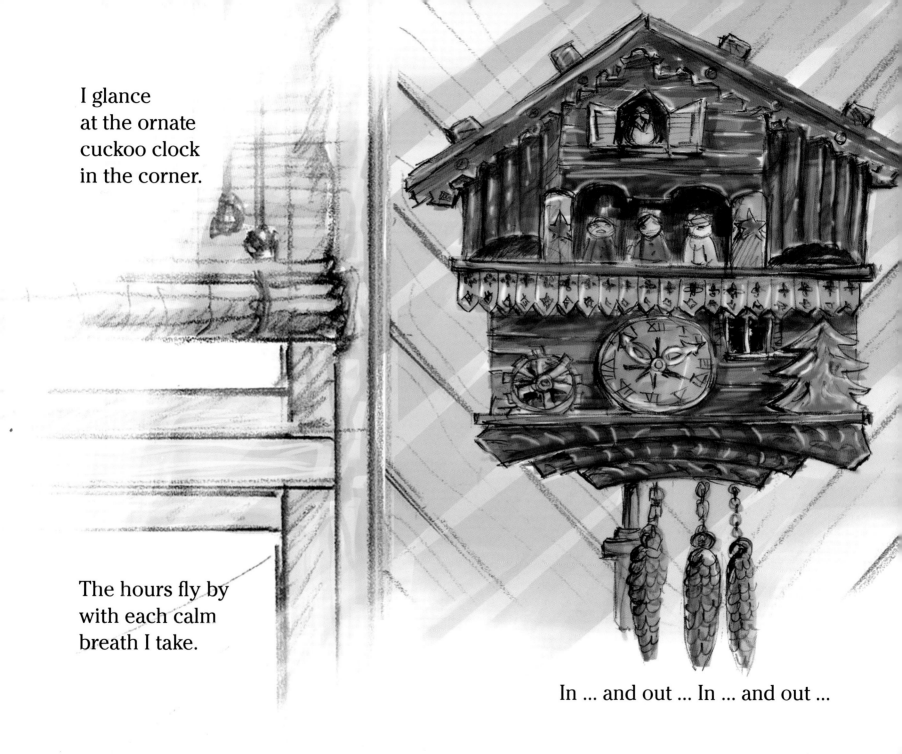

The hours fly by
with each calm
breath I take.

In ... and out ... In ... and out ...

I nestle into Grandma's knobby sofa chair. The marching
band in my head plays a wretched tune. I'm burning up.

Steam rises from the bowl of chicken soup on the rickety TV table beside my chair. It smells delicious and comforting. I reach for the warm bowl. It overpowers the pounding within.

Pasta bowties float into each spoonful of warm broth.
The hearty stock fills my belly.

"The Price is Right" jingle plays on the television. "Come on down!"

Grandma's TV is an antique. I time the buzzing zaps that interrupt the program.

Grandma musically scours the aluminum pan free from chicken scraps.

The swish of her bedroom slippers grows louder as she scurries across the linoleum.

I drop the afghan to
the floor and make
my way to the living
room. The hands
of the cherry wood
grandfather clock
at the bottom of the
staircase are near the
stroke of three.

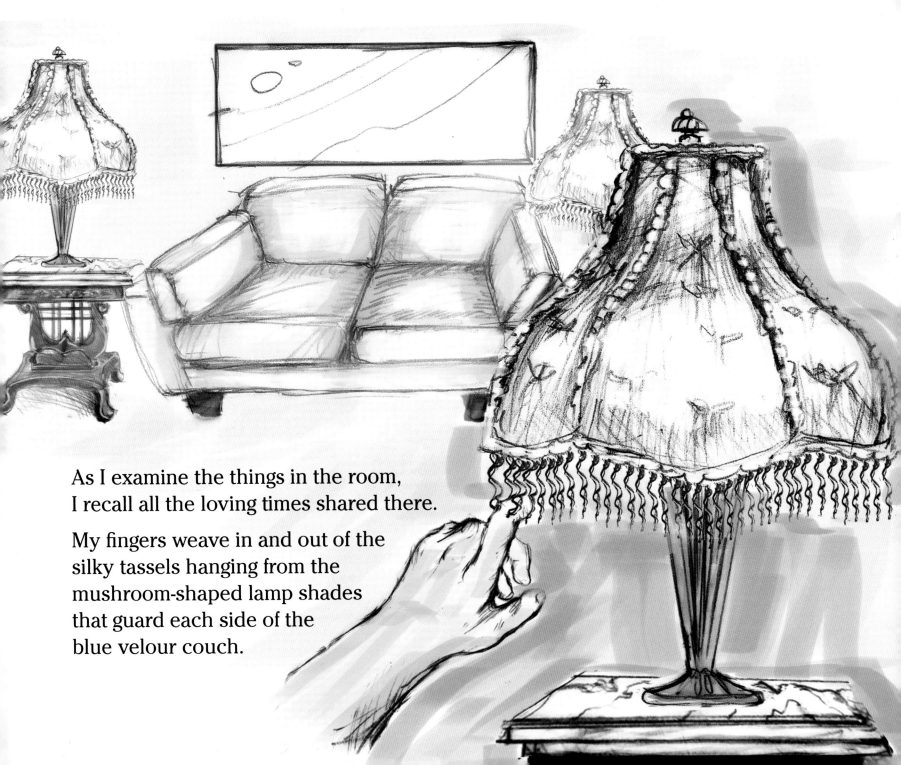

As I examine the things in the room,
I recall all the loving times shared there.

My fingers weave in and out of the
silky tassels hanging from the
mushroom-shaped lamp shades
that guard each side of the
blue velour couch.

The artist's chair—at least that's what I call it—comes into view with the sunlight shining on it through the bow window. The chair has an awkward shape, almost perfectly designed to display the human form.

The extended wooden arch on one side of the cushioned back gently tapers down to the other, like an expert skier's finest slope. I place myself in a pose that fits the curves of the chair and close my eyes.

My cousin, Donna, sits at the piano and rhythmically shares
"Jingle Bell Rock." I hear wrapping paper crumpling as
my brother and I tear the wrapping paper
off of our gifts, one strip at a time.

The brick fireplace houses crackling logs, whose flames dance in the marble hearth ...

... keeping the most warm-hearted family cozy on a bitterly cold Christmas day.

Grandma's jolly chuckle fills the living room; it's the vibrant heart of the atmosphere.

I linger a little longer in the entrance way at the bottom of the staircase, clinging to the wooden spiral banister. Dad will be picking me up soon. I don't want to let go of the aromatic essence of Grandma's house.

Is it from the chicken soup? The stuffed artichokes she made two nights ago? Years of stale smoke hibernating in the drapery? The cooling Shower-to-Shower powder wafting from beneath the silky layer of her blouse?

I realize its origin is not important. I would always savor it.

And to my surprise, it would overcome my senses again twenty years later when I walk into my parents' house after a long absence.

I am thankful for our senses.
They keep our memories
alive forever.